```
FRIONA JUNIOR HIGH SCHOOL LIB
15118      797.2 HOL
           Snorkeling
```

ADVENTURERS

SNORKELING

Mike Holbrook

CRESTWOOD HOUSE
New York

First Crestwood House edition 1993
© Julian Holland Publishing Ltd 1993

First published by Heinemann Library 1993, an imprint of Heinemann Educational, a division of Heinemann Publishers (Oxford) Ltd, Halley Court, Jordan Hill, Oxford OX2 8EJ

All rights reserved. No part of this publication may be reproduced or transmitted in any form or by any means, electronic or mechanical, including photocopying, recording, or by any information storage and retrieval system, without permission in writing from the Publisher.

Crestwood House
Macmillan Publishing Company
866 Third Avenue
New York, NY 10022

First edition

Macmillan Publishing Company is part of the Maxwell Communications Group of Companies.

Design by Julian Holland Publishing Ltd

Printed in Hong Kong

1 2 3 4 5 6 7 8 9 10

Library of Congress Cataloging-in-Publication Data
Holbrook, Mike.
    Snorkeling/Mike Holbrook.
      p. cm.—(Adventurers)
    Includes index.
    Summary: provides information about how to go snorkeling. It explains techniques, accessories, and safe practices required when in the water.
    ISBN 0-89686-823-0
    1. Skin diving—Juvenile literature. I. Title. II. Series.
GV840.S78H65 1994
797.2'3—dc20   92-45219

Acknowledgments
Illustrations: Lawrie Taylor
Photographs: b = below
All photographs were taken by Mike Busuttili except:
22, 23b, 35, Mike Holbrook; 38b, Mary Tetley; 39, Sea & Sea Ltd.

Thanks go to Tim Wormald for his helpful comments on the manuscript.

> **Note to the reader**
> In this book there are some words in the text which are printed in **bold** This shows that the word is listed in the glossary on pages 46–47. The glossary gives a brief explanation of words that may be new to you.

Contents

The lure of snorkeling	4
Basic equipment	6
The need for training	8
Basic physics	10
The body in water	12
Breath-hold diving	14
Basic technique in the pool	16
Protective clothing	20
Buoyancy aids	22
Snorkeling in open water	24
Surface dives	26
Signals	28
Accessories	30
Basic rescue	32
Safety in open water	34
Sea conditions	36
Snorkeling activities	38
Marine life	40
Subaqua diving	42
Diving equipment	44
International associations	46
Glossary	46
Index	48

The lure of snorkeling

Snorkeling is a sport that combines swimming on the surface and **breath-hold diving**. After a few hours of instruction in the use of mask, fins and snorkel from an experienced instructor, you will be able to observe the reefs and marine life that surround the shores while remaining on the surface. As your ability and confidence improve, brief surface dives can be made to bring you even closer to a new and wonderful world of adventure. Learning to snorkel is an ideal way to explore the shallow waters around our coasts. When you consider that over 71 percent of the earth's surface is covered by water, there are many opportunities to develop interests in marine life, and in the need for its protection and conservation. Some snorkeling activities are competitive, such as **octopush**, **aqualacrosse** and **fin swimming**, but for the vast majority of snorkelers, the sport is enjoyed at a more moderate and leisurely pace.

Snorkeling is a shared experience

A shared experience

Snorkeling is best enjoyed with a partner or in groups; apart from the safety aspect, there is always somebody to share your experiences with when you return to shore. The sport can encourage groups with a common interest to form, like identifying and recording marine life or underwater photography. Snorkeling with a purpose — and with friends who have a similar interest — is an excellent way to enjoy the sport. With the correct instruction and technique, snorkeling can be enjoyed by all ages, while providing gentle exercise and improving physical fitness.

A helping hand

Safety first

The ability to swim is essential for any sport in the water. Snorkeling can be challenging, so you need to be reasonably healthy and active before venturing too far off shore. Using fins can camouflage poor swimming ability and can lead to a false sense of security. The accidental loss of a fin while snorkeling will reduce you to being a normal swimmer, and your safe return to shore will depend on your ability to swim. If you are a weak swimmer, you will need to practice in the safety of a swimming pool.

Learning to snorkel safely in open water requires more than just being able to use the equipment. You will need to understand the effects of pressure on your body before attempting a surface dive, and how to clear your mask, should it become accidentally flooded. Poor finning technique can also reduce your performance and expend unnecessary energy. An experienced instructor is essential to help you understand the theory and practical skills and to show you the correct techniques.

Basic equipment

The mask

You will need a diving mask which will allow you to see clearly underwater, fins to enable you to move easily through the water and a snorkel tube so that you can breathe on the surface of the water with your head submerged. Mask, fins and snorkel form your **basic equipment**. A diving mask provides an air pocket so that you can see clearly underwater. It is essential that this air pocket also encloses the nose, because as you descend, the surrounding water pressure increases, and you will need to equalize the pressure by allowing air into the mask through the nose. It is very important that all diving masks provide external access to pinch the nose when ear clearing (see page 13).

The snorkel

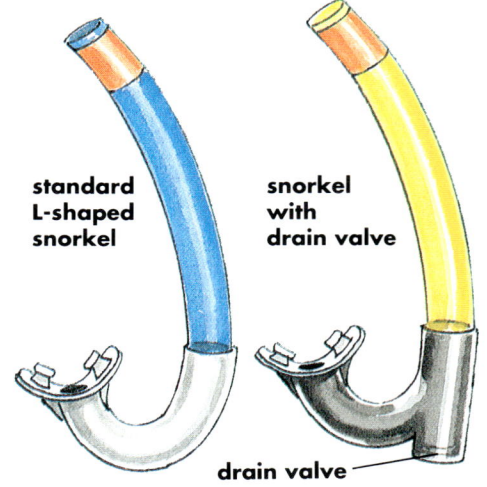

A snorkel consists of a mouthpiece and a semirigid plastic tube, and is usually curved. Some are fitted with **drain valves**, which enable you to exhale water from the snorkel while using very little effort. Valves fitted to the top or open end of the tube should be avoided.

Fins

Fins give you the ability to move on the surface and underwater using far less effort than you would expend swimming. Good finning technique allows you to move through the water using leg action alone. Fins can propel you through the water at great speed but this is not normally their main purpose.

Fins have two main parts: a soft rubber foot area and a blade made from stiff **polymer**. Shoe-type fins enclose the whole foot, whereas adjustable fins have open backs with adjustable straps and require hard-soled **neoprene** boots to be worn. Masks, fins and snorkels come in a variety of shapes and colors.

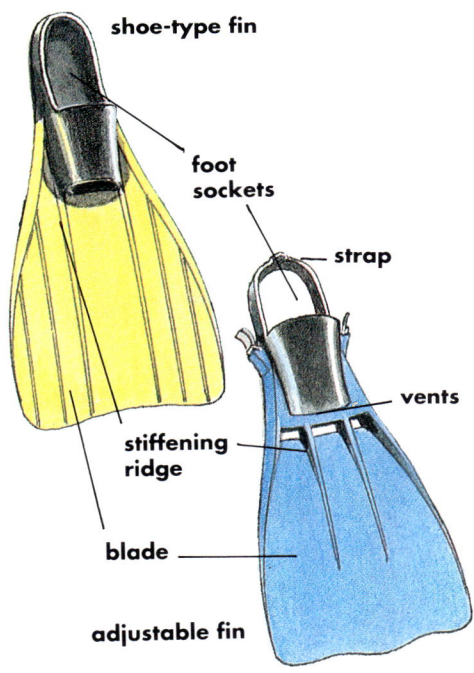

Color-coordinated basic equipment

Safety first

● Ordinary glass can break easily; always choose a mask that has a **lens** made from **tempered/toughened glass**.
● Avoid using swimming **goggles** for snorkel diving, as they have no facility to equalize pressure.
● Choose your basic equipment with care — seek expert advice.

The need for training

Instructor demonstrates fitting the fins

Swimming ability

As with all adventurous and active sports, snorkeling makes physical demands on the body's reserves of energy; therefore, it is important that you are sufficiently fit to meet these demands. Although fins are designed to improve your swimming efficiency, you should be able to swim at least 50 yards freestyle. Try supporting yourself by floating or treading water, without the use of fins or a **buoyancy aid** — this will help you relax and regain your normal breathing pattern following exercise. Without using a mask, you should feel comfortable putting your head underwater and opening your eyes, even though your vision will be blurred. If you are a moderate or weak swimmer, a few visits to your local swimming pool should improve your stamina, swimming technique and confidence.

Remember: Speed is not an essential element for the snorkeler, but the abilities to make brief and shallow surface dives, relax and feel at home in the water are distinct advantages.

Where to learn

The safest and easiest way to learn snorkeling is to receive instruction from an experienced instructor who has been qualified by a recognized authority. Learning snorkeling with a group of fellow adventurers and an instructor is more fun than trying to teach yourself alone. Most countries have a number of training agencies, schools or clubs that offer both **aqualung** diving and snorkeling programs that are especially designed for beginners. A typical program will include a number of theory lessons on safety and basic physics, plus a few practical sessions.

Snorkeling lessons are given in a swimming pool or sheltered open water, where you are shown how to use the equipment properly. A good instructor will ensure that skills are introduced progressively and will be able to demonstrate individual skills and correct faults before they develop. With this step-by-step instruction, your progress will be faster and more enjoyable. Following an organized program of lessons, there is usually a simple theory and practical test. If you are successful, a qualification certificate, badge and a qualification record book will be issued.

Practicing the finning action

Basic physics

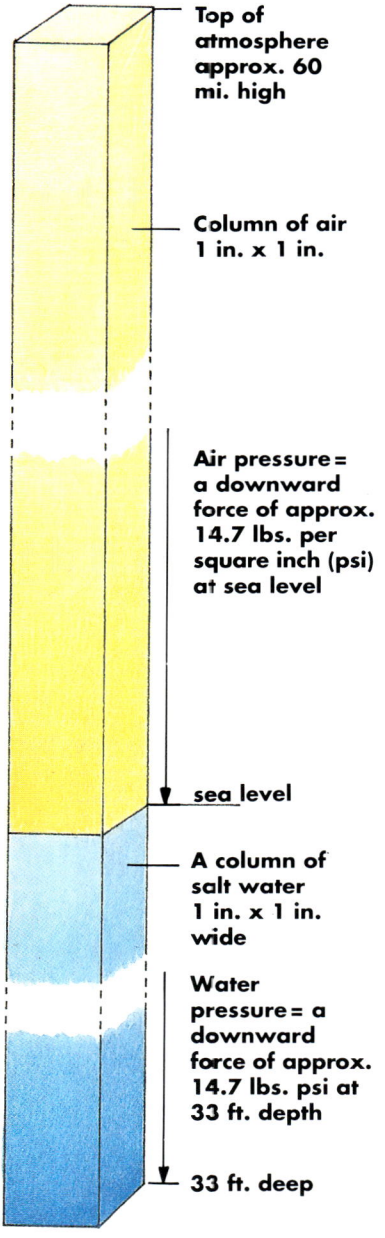

Air

The earth is surrounded by an envelope of air called the **atmosphere**. The diagram (at left) illustrates how a column of air 1 inch square extending to about 60 miles high exerts a downward pressure of approximately 14.7 lbs. per square inch at sea level — known as **atmospheric pressure** — and is expressed as 1 **bar**. Our bodies are adapted to breathing air at this pressure. We only notice pressure change when we travel in an aircraft or climb a high mountain, where reduced air pressure has an effect on our ears and breathing. Like all gases, air is compressible and can be squeezed into a smaller area by increasing its pressure.

Water

Water is virtually incompressible, dense and extremely heavy. Water pressure increases quickly with depth. For every foot of depth, the pressure increases by 0.445 psi; therefore, a snorkeler at a depth of about 11 yards would add a further 1 bar of pressure to his body. As there is already 1 bar of atmospheric pressure on the surface, he/she would be subjected to an **absolute pressure** of 2 bars – and for every further 11 yards the pressure would increase by 1 bar. Atmospheric pressure exerts downward, whereas water pressure exerts equally and in all directions. As the human body consists mainly of liquid, it can take this pressure without any decrease in volume.

Pressure/volume

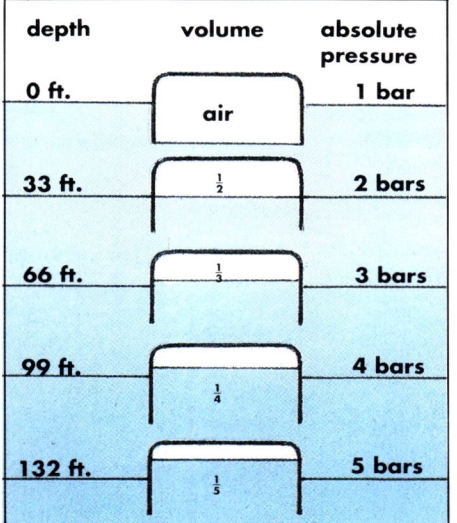

When the pressure is doubled, the volume is halved. For every 11 yards of seawater, the pressure increases by 1 bar.

The relationship between pressure and volume is known as **Boyle's law**. If you take a breath and dive to a depth of 11 yards, the air in your lungs will be compressed to one half of the original volume. The air pressure in your lungs remains equal to the surrounding water pressure. When you return to the surface, pressure falls and the air will expand to its original volume. Therefore, if the depth/pressure is doubled, the volume is halved.

Vision, light and sound

A diving mask allows you to see clearly. But because light rays bend (**refract**) when they pass from water into air, objects appear about 33 percent larger and 25 percent closer than they actually are. Light is absorbed and dispersed by particles in the water, so it becomes darker with depth. Different colors of daylight are also absorbed, so the deeper you are, the less colorful it is. Sound passes through water four times faster than in air, and it is difficult to judge its direction because of its speed.

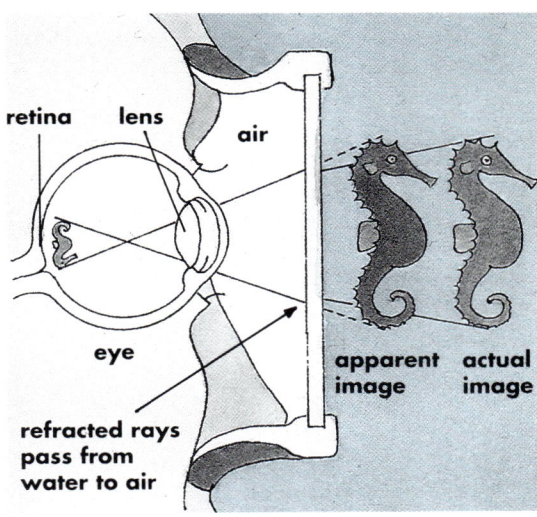

Objects appear closer and larger

11

The body in water

Buoyancy

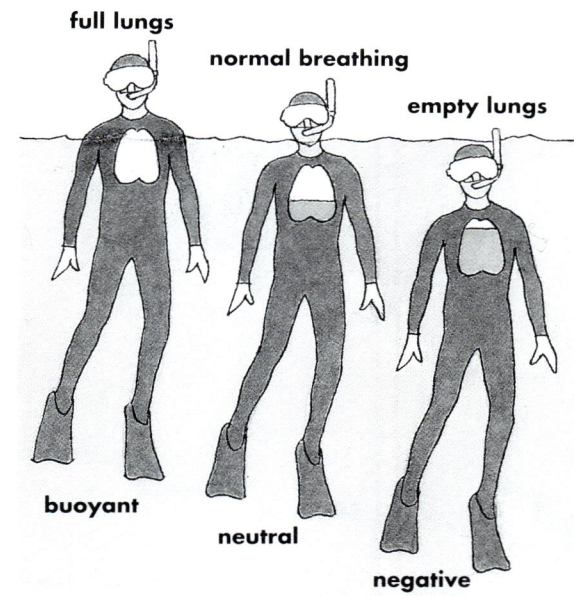

Varying the volume in your lungs can also vary your buoyancy between positive, negative and neutral

In the water with full lungs, our bodies are slightly buoyant. If we breathe out fully, we lose **buoyancy** and sink. This is due to the reduced volume of air in our lungs. If we breathe normally, we should remain static in the water; this is called neutral buoyancy, the condition we want to be. Buoyancy will be lost when you dive deeper than about 2 to 3 yards, due to increasing water pressure. You will continue to sink, unless you fin up against this negative buoyancy.

Conduction and hypothermia

In water, heat **conduction** away from the body is enormous compared to that in air. The normal body temperature is about 98.6°F. In water less than 70°F, the body will lose heat faster than it can be produced. Even in the tropics, prolonged exposure to this temperature will cause the body to chill. As the body cools, it tries to increase body heat by shivering. Further heat loss will result in the slowing down of blood flow to the extremities. The hands and feet become colder in order to conserve heat for the main organs of the body — heart, brain, et cetera. Shivering and cold hands and feet are the first signs and symptoms of **hypothermia**. If body cooling continues to about 86°F, the main organs will begin to slow down, leading to unconsciousness. Although you may feel comfortable in the water, once out, the effects of wind chill may also bring about body cooling. It's a good idea to put on a Windbreaker after a prolonged snorkel swim, to avoid further heat loss. In **temperate** waters, neoprene wetsuits are a must if you wish to stay in water for any length of time. Most of our body heat is lost through our head and hands, so keep these areas covered.

The ear

Ears are sensitive to pressure changes. Water pressure will push the **eardrum** inward in an effort to reduce the volume of middle ear air space. If this pressure continues, the eardrum can rupture. The middle ear is connected to the nose and throat by the **Eustachian tube**. By pinching the nose, closing the mouth and blowing gently against closed nostrils, air can be forced into the middle ear.

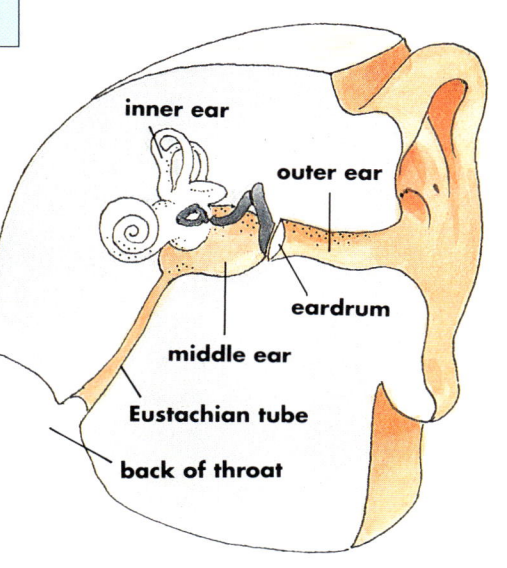

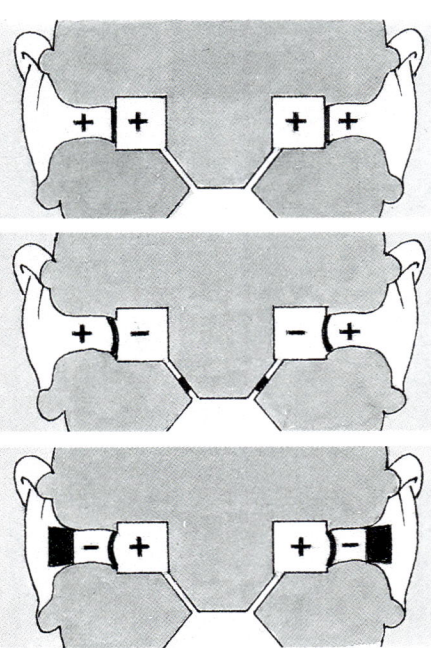

Normal eardrum (top). Eardrum distorted due to external pressure (middle). Eardrum reversed due to blocked outer ear (bottom).

This process will equalize the pressure on the eardrum and is called **ear clearing**. When diving, this method is used regularly. That is why your diving mask must have a built-in nose pocket. Sometimes your Eustachian tube may become blocked due to a cold, and you will not be able to clear your ears. If you have a cold, do not go snorkeling. The **sinuses** are also air-filled and are located in the skull. They are affected by pressure changes in the same way as the middle ear space. The act of clearing the ears will have the same effect on the sinuses.

Breath-hold diving

Effects of exercise

The air you breathe is composed of approximately 21 percent **oxygen** (O_2) and 79 percent **nitrogen** (N_2). Your body needs oxygen and food to provide energy for day-to-day exercise. When you breathe in, air enters your lungs and is diffused into the bloodstream. It is then pumped around your body via the heart to the vital organs and muscles. When you breathe out, some of the oxygen has been used (4 percent) and replaced by a waste gas called **carbon dioxide** (CO_2). This process is called metabolism and can be expressed as: food+oxygen=energy+carbon dioxide+water+waste products. The more you exercise, the more oxygen you require and the more carbon dioxide you produce. Breathing becomes deeper and faster the more you exercise.

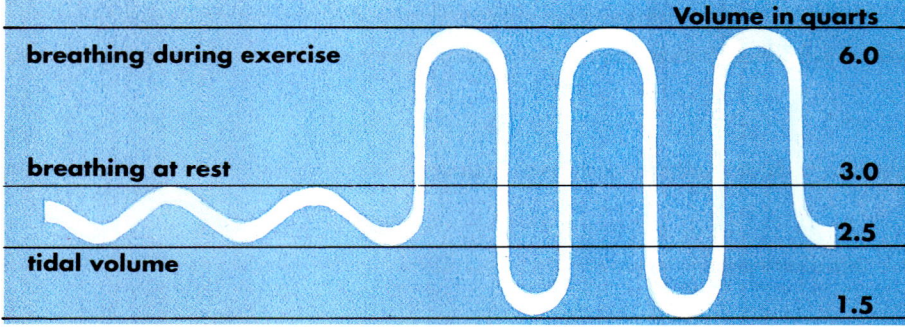

Breathing pattern during rest and exercise

Safety first

- Avoid making breath-hold dives of more than a few seconds.
- Do not ignore the desire to breathe.
- Do not try to extend your duration underwater by hyperventilating — take only a couple of breaths before diving.
- Build up your air endurance underwater by exercise and improving your fitness.
- Avoid competitions to see who can hold their breath longest underwater — the winner could stay down!
- Do not attempt surface dives if you are suffering from a cold.

Hyperventilation

The total volume of air held by the lungs varies but is usually about 6 quarts for an adult male. When exercising hard, 4.5 quarts can be breathed in and out (**vital capacity**); the remaining 1.5 quarts cannot (**residual volume**). At rest a person normally breathes in and out around 0.5 of a quart (**tidal volume**). Holding your breath interferes with the normal breathing pattern. As the body continues to use oxygen (O_2), the buildup of carbon dioxide (CO_2) triggers the desire to breathe. If this desire is deliberately over-ridden by a diver who swims too far underwater, the amount of oxygen can fall to a dangerously low level, and unconsciousness may occur.

The risk of unconsciousness can increase if the diver goes too deep. Because the pressure in the lungs is equal to the surrounding water pressure, although the volume of the lungs is decreased, the body believes it has more O_2. On ascent, the pressure in the lungs decreases, and the level of O_2 drops before the CO_2 has triggered the desire to breathe. By taking lots of very deep breaths before diving, it is possible to reduce the amount of CO_2 in the body and thereby suppress the desire to breathe. This is called **hyperventilation** and should never be attempted by the snorkeler, as it reduces CO_2 but does not increase the level of O_2 that is vital for life.

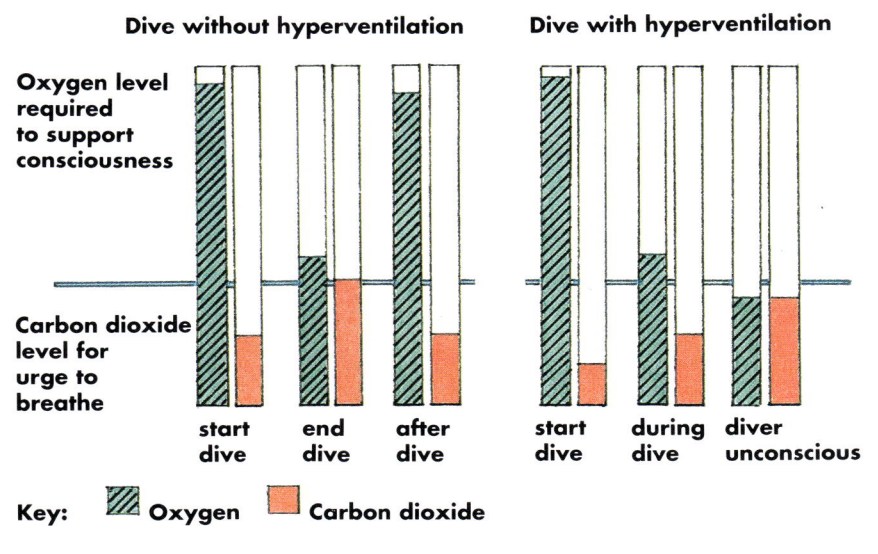

Basic technique in the pool

Putting on the fins

It is more comfortable to put on your fins while sitting at the edge of the swimming pool or standing in chest-deep water and using the pool side for support. Fold the shoe socket or heel strap underneath the foot section of the fin and push your foot into the pocket. Pull the heel strap or shoe socket up and around your ankle. Walking, running around or trying to climb up and down pool ladders while wearing fins can cause an accident. If you have to move out of the water, be careful. You will probably find it easier to shuffle sideways or walk backward. Even in shallow water, trying to walk is difficult; walking backward is easier and provides less resistance.

Putting on basic equipment by the pool

Useful tips

- Wet your fins to ease fitting.
- Before using a new mask, wash it in warm, soapy water to remove any grease left from the manufacturer.
- Store your fins flat to keep their shape.
- Keep your basic equipment out of direct sunlight, which can discolor or destroy it.
- Clean your equipment after use with fresh water and store it away from extreme temperatures.

Fitting the mask

Before fitting the mask, you will need to adjust the retaining strap so that the mask fits comfortably. Do not overtighten, as this can distort the thin seal that fits around the face and can cause leaks. You will also need to mist-proof the lens; otherwise, your vision will be blurred. Most snorkelers use saliva to mist-proof the inside of the lens and then rinse it in clean water. However, demisting solutions can be purchased for this purpose. To fit the mask, hold the rim in one hand and fold the mask strap in front of the lens. Clear away any hair from your forehead, and press the mask to your face. Hold the mask in place and, with your other hand, pull the mask strap over and around the crown of your head. You may need to make a further small adjustment of the mask strap for comfort.

Students fitting their masks

Fitting the snorkel

A snorkel is usually worn under the mask strap or attached to it by means of a snorkel-retaining loop, which is normally supplied with the snorkel. When fitting the snorkel, make sure it is angled slightly backward, so that when the head is submerged, the snorkel is vertical on the water's surface. Grip the mouthpiece lugs lightly between your teeth and fit the soft flange between your lips and front teeth. Turn or adjust the mouthpiece so that it feels comfortable in your mouth. Some snorkels can be adjusted to suit various head shapes by means of a rotating section built into the snorkel tube. If drain valves are fitted, check that the small **mushroom valve** has not been disturbed; otherwise, water will flood the snorkel, and it will be impossible to clear.

Fitting and adjusting the snorkel to the correct angle

Using mask, fins and snorkel

Snorkel clearing is an important skill to master

Fit the mask and submerge until your face and mask are covered. If water leaks in, check to see whether any hair is trapped under the mask seal and if the mask is seated properly. Any water entering the mask during snorkeling can easily be removed by bringing the head clear of the water and lifting the lower mask seal.

With the mask and snorkel fitted, hold the top of the snorkel and submerge until you feel water touching your hand. You will notice that you breathe through your mouth and not through your nose. Every time you surface dive, you will need to clear the snorkel. This is achieved by a short, forceful exhalation, and not by removing the mouthpiece.

Practice using your fins by holding onto the side of the swimming pool. Extend your legs and fin using full and deep strokes from the hips. Avoid bending your knees, as this leads to a bicycling action that is ineffective and wastes energy.

Protective clothing

Tropical

In tropical conditions, even though you feel cooler in the water than on land, the sun's rays can be very strong, and without some form of protection you could get badly sunburned. Wearing an old T-shirt will offer some protection from the sun, but has little thermal insulation.

Although the water is generally warmer in the tropics, prolonged submersion can still chill your body. Accidentally brushing against **coral** can cause cuts; some corals such as fire coral can also sting if touched. A skintight all-in-one **Lycra** suit will protect your body from the sun and provide a little warmth. It will also protect you from scratches and coral cuts. Gloves provide added protection for your hands.

An all-in-one suit offers good protection against scratches and cuts

Temperate

In temperate waters, a **wetsuit** is the most popular form of thermal protection. Wetsuits are generally made from foamed or expanded neoprene, which has gas bubbles trapped within the material. These bubbles are separated from each other by a layer of rubber, so that the material does not absorb water. Water enters the gap between the suit and the skin and soon warms to body temperature. It is insulated from the surrounding cold water by the layer of insulating bubbles. Avoid loose or poor-fitting wetsuits, as they allow too much water to circulate around the body, causing excessive chilling. Wetsuits are buoyant, so it will be necessary for you to wear a **weight belt** to counteract this additional resilience.

Snorkeler using a wetsuit jacket for thermal protection

Buying a suit

A "shorty" one-piece wetsuit has short sleeves and legs, and is generally used in warm waters or swimming pools. A typical wetsuit has pants, jacket, hood and slippers, which gives you the option of wearing only part of the suit in warmer water.

Although wetsuits need to be close fitting, avoid suits that are too tight, as this will restrict your movements in the water. Choose wetsuits that are brightly colored, as they will make you more conspicuous in open water.

Buoyancy aids

Life jackets

It is strongly recommended that snorkelers wear lifejackets in open water. A **life jacket** or **buoyancy compensator** is put on over the head and fastened by a strap or harness around the waist. In an emergency, the jacket can be inflated by using a disposable **CO_2 cartridge**, which is activated by a pull cord. For non-emergencies or buoyancy adjustment, they can be inflated through a flexible mouth inflation tube that has a simple valve attached to the open end. This valve is also used for deflating the jacket after use. Life jackets are designed to support you face upward on the surface and work on the principle of displacing water with air. This increases the snorkeler's buoyancy in the water. Life jackets are normally worn deflated while snorkeling, since the increased drag of an inflated jacket could make progress through the water difficult. It is also nearly impossible to surface dive when you are wearing an inflated life jacket. Some life jackets are fitted with a whistle, which is useful for attracting attention in an emergency.

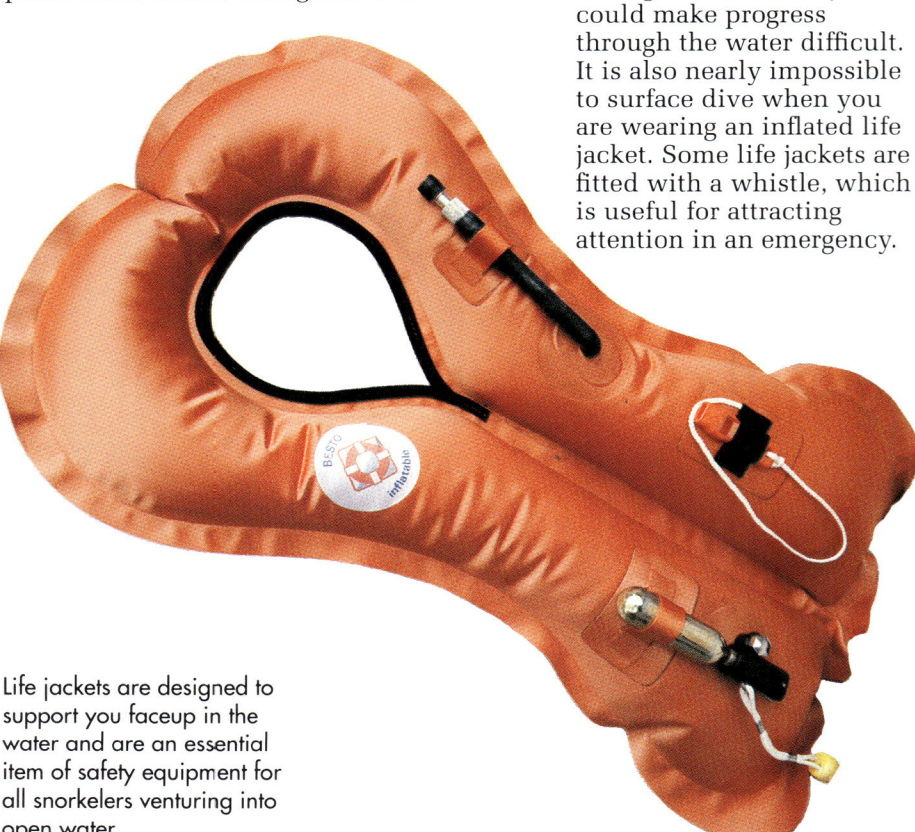

Life jackets are designed to support you faceup in the water and are an essential item of safety equipment for all snorkelers venturing into open water.

Using a life jacket

In an emergency situation, operate the pull cord on your life jacket. Remember, once you have used the cartridge in this way, you will need to buy a replacement. For safety, it is a good idea to have the cartridge and activating mechanisms checked regularly by an authorized dealer, as salt water can corrode the working parts. If you are tired or require a little extra buoyancy, use the inflator tube to inflate your jacket. While treading water, remove your snorkel and then breathe out your exhaled air into the life jacket. After two or three breaths, you should have sufficient buoyancy to relax and remain afloat.

Snorkeler with an inflated life jacket

Weight belts

Weight belt and colored lead weights

Weight belts are used to compensate for the positive buoyancy of a wetsuit or for people who are naturally more buoyant in the water. A weight belt must have a quick-release buckle so that in an emergency it can be removed quickly. The weight required will vary, but you should aim for neutral buoyancy with all your equipment fitted. Weights come in a variety of shapes and sizes.

23

Snorkeling in open water

Mask clearing underwater

Mask clearing is achieved by displacing the water with your exhaled air. To practice this skill, kneel or sit just below the surface and allow a little water to enter by lifting the lower seal. Tilt your head backward and press the top of the mask against your forehead, exhaling gently through your nose. Initially, more than one attempt may be necessary.

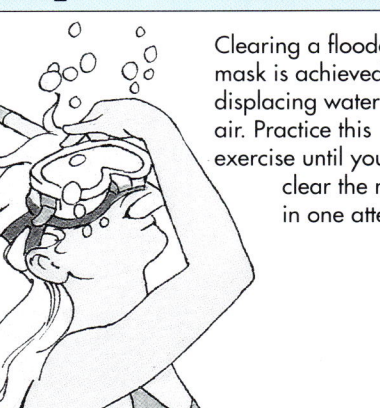

Clearing a flooded mask is achieved by displacing water with air. Practice this exercise until you can clear the mask in one attempt.

Rolls

Ease of movement through the water is a sign of an experienced snorkeler. As your skills develop, you will learn that maneuvering, or turning in the water, is comparatively effortless and is achieved by simply turning your body. Your mobility can be improved by practicing simple forward and backward rolls.

Forward roll

Backward roll

Forward rolls can be performed by leaving the surface of the water and bending from your waist into a tucked position. Then, using hands and arms, pull the water toward you. Backward rolls are performed in a similar way. However, instead of pulling the water toward you, force yourself around by pushing the water away from you. To avoid falling off a roll sideways, you should apply an equal amount of force to both arms. As your confidence improves, more than one roll can be attempted.

Surface dives

A well-performed surface dive should carry you down 2 to 3 yards. Lying face down on the surface with your arms straight out in front of you, take a breath through the snorkel, bend your body at your waist and point your arms downward (as if to touch your fins). At the same time, raise your legs upward, clear of the water. The weight of your legs will force you underwater. Try to keep your arms and legs in a straight line and do not attempt to use your fins until you are underwater. A breaststroke pull with your arms will further assist your descent. Once underwater, finning is more effective, and you can travel a long way in only a few seconds. Remember, as you descend you will experience the effects of pressure, and you will need to clear your ears and equalize the pressure in your mask.

A surface dive should be a smooth transition from surface to underwater

Surfacing procedure

Begin your ascent by looking toward the surface. Fin gently upward while looking around and above you, to avoid surfacing under another snorkeler or obstruction. In poor visibility, keep one hand held above your head, so that you can ward off any surface obstruction and reduce the chance of hitting your head. On the surface, clear your snorkel and look around to check that you have surfaced in a safe area. The more experienced snorkeler will be able to clear her snorkel as she nears the surface. Just before the surface, tilt your head backward, so that the snorkel points downward, and exhale gently. This procedure is called **displacement clearing** and helps to displace the water. Once on the surface, bring your head forward and continue clearing any remaining water from the snorkel.

A controlled ascent

Safety first

- Always practice surface dives in shallow water before going into deeper water.
- Never ignore the desire to breathe.
- Do not try to extend your time underwater by hyperventilating.
- Remember to clear your ears and equalize the pressure in your mask every time you descend.
- In clear waters, the seabed can appear nearer than it actually is.
- Always wear a life jacket in open water.
- Wear protective clothing in warm tropical waters, and a wetsuit in colder waters.
- While surfacing, keep looking up to avoid hitting an obstruction or another snorkeler!

Signals

Information signals

Signals are a more effective way of communicating than trying to talk in the water. Removing your snorkel to talk is not recommended, as water can accidentally enter your mouth and lead to distress. Signals used to communicate information or indicate direction, are generally nonmoving signals.

"OK at the surface": Given and acknowledged to the shore cover or buddy following a surface dive and means all is well.

"Stop, stay where you are": (left) This signal is usually followed by another signal explaining why, unless the reason is obvious.

"Go up, I am going up": (left) An instruction to ascend. Upward movement of the hand adds emphasis.

"Go down, I am going down": (left) An instruction to descend, normally made only at the start of a dive.

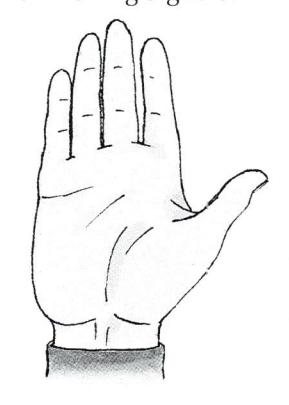

"OK, all is well": (right) This signal can be either a question from one snorkeler to another or an affirmative reply to this question.

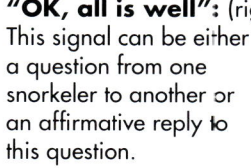

"You or me": (left) The snorkeler points to someone, showing the person referred to in the next signal.

"Something is wrong": (above) Not an emergency, but an indication that all is not well.

Emergency signals

Signals can also be used to indicate distress or an emergency. Unlike information signals, they are generally moving signals. The waving of an arm or the absence of any sign of movement should be considered as an emergency requiring immediate assistance from the buddy or shore cover (see page 34). If you go snorkeling in different countries, always check that the signals being used are understood by both snorkelers and shore cover.

"Distress at the surface – come and get me": Demands immediate action to help the distressed snorkeler.

"I am out of breath": Your buddy indicates her labored breathing by to-and-fro movements of the hands.

"Distress underwater": This signal requires immediate action to rescue the snorkeler giving it.

Snorkelers exchanging the OK signal

Accessories

Diving knife

Growing hazards for all water users are discarded ropes, nets and fishing lines that float on or below the surface. **Monofilament** line is almost impossible to see until you become snagged. To avoid being entangled, steer clear of popular fishing areas where lost lines are more likely, and for safety wear a diving knife.

Diving knives come in a variety of shapes and sizes. For the snorkeler, a small knife incorporating a line cutter and a serrated edge for cutting through large-diameter rope is probably the best option. Knives are generally fitted to the leg or upper arm with rubber straps and retained in the sheath by a rubber loop.

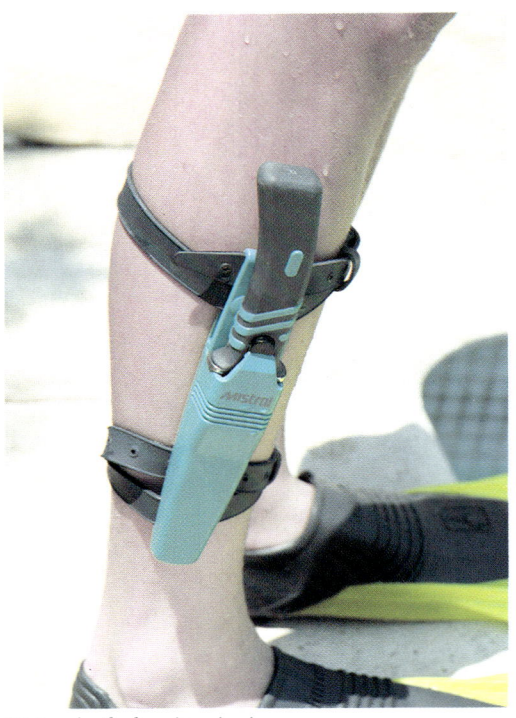
Diving knife fitted to the leg

An underwater depth gauge

Depth gauge

A **depth gauge** is a curved tube sealed at one end and open to the water at the other. Increased water pressure, acting on the trapped air in the tube, tends to make it straighten. This movement is sent via cogs to a calibrated dial.

Watches

All watches used in or under the water must be waterproof. Choose a watch that has a large clear face and preferably a long rubber strap, so that it can fit over your wetsuited wrist. Divers' watches usually incorporate a **rotating bezel**, which allows you to record elapsed time. This feature is of more benefit to the aqualung diver than to the snorkeler.

A waterproof watch with a clear face

Floats & reels

A brightly colored float with a diver's **"A" flag** fitted to the top gives a visible warning to other water users. Floats can also be a source of additional buoyancy for tired or exhausted snorkelers. Inflatable floats have the advantage of being more portable when not being used. Because they are light, they may require small lead weights fitted underneath to keep them upright in the water. Using the float, line and reel as a buddy line may be useful to keep a group together on the surface. Remember to reel your line in as you ascend so that you do not become entangled.

Floats should be brightly colored and visible to other water users. Inflatable floats are generally more portable.

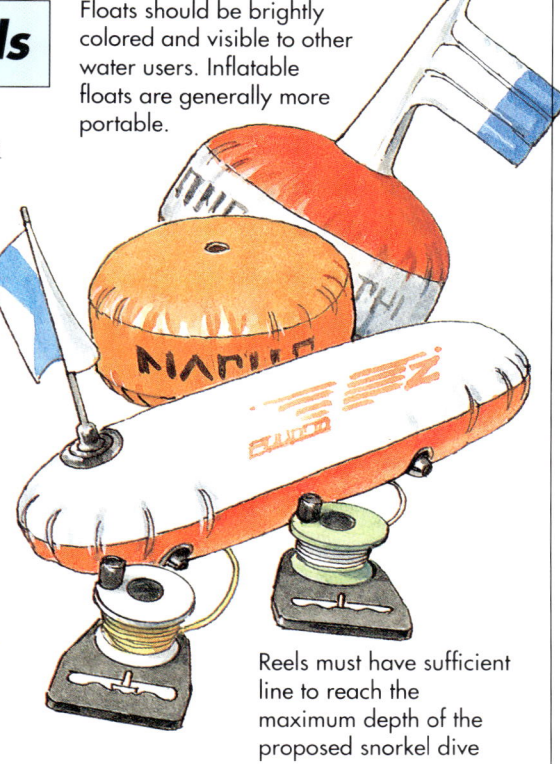

Reels must have sufficient line to reach the maximum depth of the proposed snorkel dive

Basic rescue

Cramp

Lack of snorkeling practice or excessive exertion may contribute to a contraction of the calf muscles, the toes or the instep known as cramp. If this occurs while snorkeling, stop finning and try to relax. The pain can often be relieved by stretching and massaging the affected muscle, although in the water this can prove difficult to perform on your own. Assistance from your buddy is usually the best solution. Clearly, if the pain continues, you may need to be towed back to safety by your buddy, where you can rest the affected muscle.

Self-help

Regular practice and keeping fit are important elements in being able to deal effectively with the occasional incident. Wear a life jacket at all times and protect yourself in cold water with a wetsuit. If you feel ill at ease in the water, or the sea conditions are less than ideal, then return to shore. Finning long distances can be tiring and may lead to breathlessness. In this situation, stop, inflate your life jacket and regain control of your breathing. Plan your snorkeling activities so that you are able to return to shore easily.

What to do in an emergency

Incidents can occur even if you have taken all precautions. They can begin as minor incidents — a lost fin or leaking mask — and, if left unattended, can develop into serious emergencies. Always keep an eye on your buddy for signs that he/she is ill at ease. Usually, inflating your buddy's life jacket will be sufficient to restore confidence and overcome his/her distress. If he/she continues to show distress, it may be necessary to remove his/her weight belt and tow him/her to safety.

Inflate your life jacket if you are feeling tired

Towing

A conscious casualty should be towed from behind, the rescuer finning backward and keeping a secure grip on the casualty's life jacket. In this position the rescuer can fin without kicking the casualty. During the tow, the rescuer should check his/her direction. With an unconscious casualty, it is essential that **expired air resuscitation (EAR)** be administered immediately. EAR, also known as the kiss of life, is a simple and effective way of ventilating the lungs and can be given anywhere, even in water! (It is recommended that all water users attend an approved training course in this essential lifesaving technique.)

To be effective, EAR requires a clear airway to the lungs; tilting the head backward extends the neck and opens the airway. The rescuer then seals the casualty's nose and exhales through the mouth. In water it is easier to close the mouth and exhale through the nose. Initially 2 breaths should be given and then at a rate of 12 to 16 breaths per minute. Clearly, towing and performing EAR at the same time can be very tiring. It is important for the rescuer to adjust his/her pace to avoid overexertion. Continue with EAR throughout the tow and landing, and until qualified medical assistance can be summoned.

Tow the casualty on your back, using an extended arm tow

Safety in open water

One up — one down

While snorkeling, buddy divers should remain in close contact with each other. This is especially important when you make a breath-hold dive. Always have a buddy on the surface who can observe your dive and act as safety cover. The practice of "one up, one down" ensures that there is always someone available to give assistance on the surface or during the ascent. Having a second snorkeler ready to help can often prevent a minor incident from developing into an emergency.

One up, one down for safety

Safety first

● Before entering the water, check the weather and sea conditions.
● Obtain local knowledge about the direction and strength of **currents**. You may be faced with finning back against a strong current.
● Check your entry and exit points. A change of tide may mean that on your return, the water has dropped and your exit is too high and dangerous.
● Agree beforehand with your buddy or group on the direction to be taken and on the approximate time of your return.
● Keep a good lookout for other water users, particularly water-skiers and fast-moving craft.
● Always check your equipment before entering the water.

Shore cover

It makes sense to tell somebody where you are going and how long you are likely to be gone. Using shore cover means there is always someone to come to your assistance in an emergency, or to alert the emergency services. Keeping a careful watch from shore can be difficult if the snorkelers are some distance off or about to disappear around a headland. The shore cover may have to follow the snorkelers along the shoreline in order to maintain visible contact. A brightly colored surface float is a useful and visible object that makes monitoring easier for the lookout. A regular exchange of "OK" signals between snorkelers and shore cover adds to the safety of those in the water. A pair of binoculars is also useful.

Other water users

Swimmers in the water are not easily seen by large vessels or fast-moving speedboats. Other water users also enjoy sports like water-skiing and powerboat racing. Fortunately, the most interesting marine life exists around the shallow and rocky coastline, where snorkeling is relatively safe compared to the open sea. If you are unable to avoid congested areas, use a conspicuous surface float with an "A" flag fitted to the top and make sure there is always a good lookout. Brightly colored protective clothing can make you more visible in the water. Remember, do not assume you have been seen — take avoiding action early!

Keep well away from surface craft and keep a lookout

Sea conditions

Tropical

It would be wrong to assume that tropical conditions always mean warm and calm seas. Sea conditions throughout the world are affected by the weather. Although other factors like **tidal streams** and pollution influence sea conditions, it is the wind direction and its strength that have most effect. Wind traveling over large areas of ocean builds up rough seas on exposed coasts or isolated islands. Waves can build up quickly, making snorkeling difficult and dangerous, particularly when you are tossed close to sharp and dangerous coral reefs. The tropics have some of the most enjoyable snorkeling conditions in the world. Coral reefs around the world attract large numbers of snorkelers and aqualung divers. The abundance and beauty of the marine life in crystal-clear water is a delight to underwater photographers and marine biologists. The Red Sea, the Caribbean islands, Australia's Great Barrier Reef and islands in the Indian Ocean are among the most exotic areas in the world for diving and snorkeling. However, all these areas suffer from tropical storms and hurricanes, which can develop quickly.

Coral reefs are popular with snorkelers and aqualung divers

Corals have a multitude of colors and different shapes

Temperate

Although temperate waters are colder and lack the deep blue of the tropics, the seas around Europe can be remarkably clear but generally have a green color due to the amount of nutrients in the water. Few corals exist, but many forms of seaweed flourish, providing a rich habitat for marine life. You will need thermal protection in temperate waters, but this will not stop you from enjoying the variety of underwater life. The Mediterranean usually has clear water and good sea temperatures during the summer months. Although here, again, seasonal winds can change the sea conditions very quickly.

Snorkeling vacations

Most destinations that are frequented by aqualung divers will also prove equally suitable for the snorkeler. Equipment rental should be relatively inexpensive, as you may only need to rent a weight belt and weights. Snorkeling vacations are usually advertised in magazines for aqualung divers. The easiest way to travel is to join a local snorkeling club that organizes regular snorkeling trips to various destinations.

Snorkeling activities

Games

Snorkeling skills can be improved and developed in watersports such as octopush, fin swimming and aqualacrosse, which are all highly competitive and are played on an international level. Octopush was invented in England by Alan Blake in 1954 and has become one of the most popular underwater sports. Using basic equipment, players attempt to score goals by pushing a **"squid"** underwater and into the opposition's goal. Fin swimmers race, using a large single fin with two foot pockets into which the feet are placed. Very fast speeds can be achieved on and under the surface. Aqualacrosse is a swimming pool version of the field game lacrosse, where opposing teams attempt to score goals. Unlike octopush, aqualacrosse is played mainly on the surface.

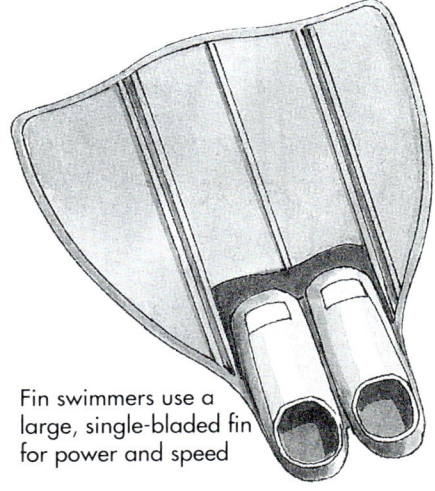

Fin swimmers use a large, single-bladed fin for power and speed

Aqualacrosse is a pool version of the field game lacrosse

Underwater photography

Underwater photography has become a popular and rewarding snorkeling activity. Modern underwater cameras have a strong waterproof housing and lens. Some cameras have a limited depth range but produce very acceptable results — ideal for the snorkeler to record a snorkeling vacation. Lack of light is a major problem in anything other than crystal-clear visibility. However, most cameras have flash units built in or attached to the housing. Using a flash will restore color to your photograph. Close-up attachments can also be fitted. They will enable you to focus in on subjects at very close range. In poor visibility, close-up frames are widely used but require a flash for best results.

Even with limited experience, the snorkeler can produce excellent underwater pictures using modern all-in-one cameras. On the right is a modern waterproof camera with built-in flash and 35-mm lens.

watertight camera housing

built-in flash unit

lens

Marine life

Tropical waters

Few things are more overwhelming to snorkelers on a first visit to a coral reef than the enormous variety of fish life visible just below the surface. Identifying various species in this bewildering array of fish and marine life is often baffling. Angel-, trigger- and butterfly fish are some of the most dazzling of reef dwellers. While larger fish like groupers live in holes or caverns and wait for appetizing meals to drift by, the parrot fish nibble on corals with their strong teeth.

Corals are living animals — polyps — which feed on **plankton** and small sea creatures. The coral reefs are the skeletons of these coral polyps. Corals grow in a variety of shapes and colors, both soft and hard. Some hard corals are descriptively named, such as elkhorn, staghorn and brain coral. Soft corals look like exotic plants and add enormous color to the reef. Some soft corals grow into giant fans of red, green and yellow, which sway gently in the current, while others resemble baskets large enough to hold a snorkeler!

You can buy waterproof plastic cards that name and show colorful pictures of the most common fish and corals that you might see when snorkeling in the area.

Fish on a coral reef

Blue parrot fish among hard and soft coral

Temperate water

Marine life in temperate waters is less diverse than that in tropical waters, but the number of each species is usually greater. Various types of seaweed (kelp) form dense forests in the shallower coastal areas. Temperate waters are rich in plankton, which form the basis of the food chain. Drifting plankton can considerably reduce the water visibility during certain times of the year, as they rise from deep water toward the sunlight.

Exploring the coastal areas will reveal lobsters, edible crabs and crawfish that hide in cracks and holes. Sea urchins and starfish occupy the sandy areas, with flat fish like sole and flounder. Seals may accompany the snorkeler on his/her journey along the coast.

Dangerous fish

In general, animals will defend themselves. When disturbed in their lairs, they can become aggressive if provoked. Jellyfish and fire coral can inflict severe pain to exposed parts of the body, so gloves and protective clothing should be worn. If you walk over shallow reefs in bare feet you can step on the spines of stonefish or sea urchins. Always wear boots and shuffle your feet when entering the water, so that you disturb anything that is buried under the sand. While underwater, it is safer for you to avoid touching anything.

Subaqua diving

The need for training

Snorkel diving provides a brief opportunity to explore the underwater world. You may wish to stay underwater longer and descend deeper. To do this, you will need to use an **aqualung**. Most, if not all, of your snorkeling skills will give you a flying start, as they are all essential for aqualung diving. Like learning to snorkel, it is important to receive the correct training from a recognized diver-training agency that uses qualified and experienced instructors. There are new skills to learn and more knowledge to gain before you can dive safely in open water.

Along with practical lessons in the swimming pool and sheltered water, you will also learn about the effects that prolonged submersion has on the body. You will learn how to assemble and use your equipment safely. Your existing rescue skills will be built upon to include rescue from deep water and buddy-monitoring skills. Using an aqualung underwater for the first time will amaze the diver — you will be able to stay down without having to surface for another breath!

Instructor and student enjoying the underwater world

Using an aqualung enables you to explore longer and deeper

Where to learn

Diver-training agencies exist in most countries; it is important to be trained by a recognized organization. Some are club-based, and training is conducted at a pace to suit your individual ability. Diving schools are able to offer concentrated programs of instruction either at a resort or near your hometown. Responsible agencies will require potential divers to undergo a medical, which includes a chest X ray so that any disqualifying factors can be spotted early, before you invest in equipment and time. Training should progress from sheltered water to open water, much the same as for your snorkel lessons.

Safety first

● Do not teach yourself aqualung diving.
● Choose a nationally recognized agency.
● Instruction should be given by a qualified diving instructor, with lots of open-water experience.
● Diving with an aqualung without the necessary skills and knowledge can be dangerous and may cost you your life.
● Most diving clubs and schools have introductory sessions that enable you to sample the sport. Always ask about these.

43

Diving equipment

The aqualung

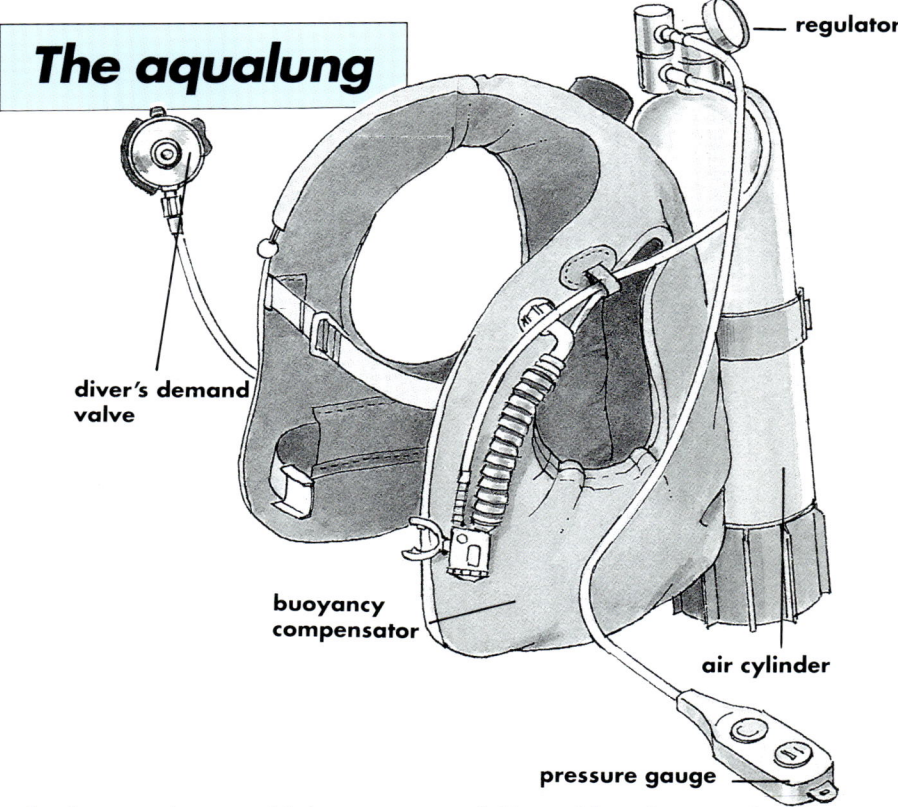

Cylinder, regulator and life jacket/harness are collectively referred to as the aqualung. The diver's air supply is contained in a high-pressure cylinder that is usually made from steel or aluminum alloy. Cylinders are available in a variety of sizes. The air pressure in the cylinder can be around 230 bars, or one hundred times more than the pressure in a normal car tire! The regulator, which is fitted to the cylinder, reduces this high-pressure air to the surrounding water pressure (**ambient pressure**), and the air is delivered by a hose to the diver through the mouth-held demand valve. The regulator also includes a **cylinder pressure gauge**, so that the diver can monitor the air supply during the dive. Modern harnesses usually incorporate the life jacket, which is secured to the cylinder with a quick-release band and straps. The diver puts on the life jacket in a similar way to putting on a normal jacket. The jacket can also be equipped with systems for inflating and deflating in an emergency or for normal buoyancy adjustment.

Diver on an underwater cliff face

International associations

Australian Underwater Federation
 (AUF)
P.O. Box 1006, Civic Square
Australian Capitol Territories
 (ACT) 2608
Australia

The British Sub-Aqua Club
 & BSAC Schools
Telford's Quay, Ellesmere Port
Cheshire L65 4FY, UK

BSAC JAPAN
Mycal Group
Building 8-5-30
Akasaka, Minato-ku
Tokyo 107, Japan

Confédération Mondiale des
 Activités Subaquatiques (CMAS)
World Underwater Federation
Viale Tiziano 70
Rome 00196, Italy

National Association of Underwater
 Instructors (NAUI)
P.O. Box 14650
Montclair, California 91763

New Zealand Underwater
 Federation (NZUF)
30 Orakei Road
Renvera, Auckland, New Zealand

Professional Association of Diving
 Instructors (PADI)
1251 East Dyer Road #100
Santa Ana, California 92705

Sub-Aqua Association
Bryslan House, Upper Street, Fleet
Hampshire GU13 9PE, UK

Scuba Schools International (SSI)
2619 Canton Court
Fort Collins, Colorado 80525

YMCA
6083A Oakbrook Parkway
Norcross, Georgia 30093

Glossary

"A" flag: international code of signals flag: "I have a diver down; keep clear at slow speed"
absolute pressure: the total pressure — on a diver this is atmospheric pressure plus water pressure
ambient pressure: pressure at any given depth
aqualacrosse: a swimming-pool version of lacrosse
aqualung: collective term for a diver's regulator, life jacket/harness and cylinder
atmosphere: the layer of air that surrounds the earth
atmospheric pressure: air pressure exerts a downward force; at sea level, this is measured as being 1 bar
bar: describes the earth's atmospheric pressure at sea level
basic equipment: collective term for mask, fins and snorkel
Boyle's law: the relationship between pressure/volume. An inverted, open-ended container full of air at the surface will appear half full of air at a depth of 11 yards — when the pressure is doubled, the volume is halved

breath-hold diving: a dive from the surface while holding your breath
buoyancy: the ability to float
buoyancy aid: any object that provides buoyancy, i.e., allows you to float
buoyancy compensator: a flotation jacket styled like a vest that can be inflated by the user
carbon dioxide: a gaseous waste product of metabolism; 4 percent of exhaled air
CO_2 cartridge: a small cylinder filled with carbon dioxide
conduction: heat transmission from an area of high temperature to one of lower temperature; e.g. from the body to the water
corals: hard or soft substances built up by marine polyps
currents: moving body of water in a known direction
cylinder pressure gauge: fitted to a diver's regulator; measures the pressure of air within an aqualung cylinder
depth gauge: an instrument for indicating depth by measuring water pressure
displacement clearing: a technique used on ascent for displacing water with air from the snorkel tube
drain valve: fitted to some snorkels to ease clearing of water
ear clearing: a technique used for equalizing the pressure on both sides of the eardrum
eardrum: internal membrane of the ear
Eustachian tube: a tube connecting the back of the throat to the middle ear; used in ear clearing
expired air resuscitation (EAR): a technique used to ventilate an unconscious victim's lungs. Commonly known as "the kiss of life"
fin swimming: an internationally played competitive sport, where large, single-bladed fins are used for speed
goggles: eye protection for surface use only
hyperventilation: overbreathing in an attempt to extend underwater duration
hypothermia: a condition where the body becomes colder and colder. Vital organs slow down, leading to unconsciousness

lens: single or double-faced plate fitted to a mask
life jacket: a device for supporting a person face upward in the water
Lycra: a material made from polyester/nylon
monofilament: a strong, clear nylon line
mushroom valve: a soft, rubber, one-way device
neoprene: soft rubberlike material used to make wetsuits
nitrogen: an inert gas that forms 79 percent of the atmosphere but serves no useful purpose within the body
octopush: a competitive game played in and under the water
oxygen: forms 21 percent of the atmosphere and is vital to life
plankton: microscopic organisms found in the sea
polymer: a compound formed from a number of materials
refraction: bending of light rays passing from water to air — causes objects to appear larger and closer
residual volume: the amount of air that cannot be exhaled from the lungs
rotating bezel: a circular device fitted to a diver's watch, which manually records elapsed time
sinuses: rigid, air-filled spaces located in the skull
"squid": a wooden disk used to score goals in octopush
temperate: a climate with no extremes of heat and cold
tempered/toughened glass: shatterproof or strengthened glass for diving masks
tidal streams: horizontal movement of water caused by the rising and falling of sea level
tidal volume: amount of air breathed in and out while at rest — 0.5 quart
vital capacity: the maximum amount of air that can be breathed in and out — 4.5 quart
weight belt: a belt to which lead weights are fitted to counteract positive buoyancy
wetsuit: a neoprene suit that provides thermal insulation in the water

Index

The numbers in **bold** are illustrations

"A" flag 31, 35, 46
absolute pressure 10, **11**, 46
air 10, 14
ambient pressure 44, 46
aqualacrosse 4, 38, 46
aqualung 44, 46
atmosphere 10, 46
atmospheric pressure 10, **10**, 46

bar 10, **11**, 44, 46
basic equipment 6, **16**, 19, 46
Boyle's law 11, **11**, 46
breath-hold diving 4, 14, 15, 34, 47
buoyancy 12, **12**, 47
buoyancy aids 8, 22, 47
buoyancy compensator 22, 47

carbon dioxide 14, 15, 47
clothing 20, **20**, 21, **21**, 35, 41
compass **31**
conductivity 12, 47
corals 20, 36, 37, 40, 41, 47
cramp 32
currents 34, 47
cylinder pressure gauge 44, 47

depth gauge 30, **30**, 47
displacement clearing 27, 47
drain valve 6, **6**, 47

ear clearing 13, **13**, 47
eardrum 13, **13**, 47
ears 13, **13**
Eustachian tube 13, **13**, 47

exercise 14, **14**
expired air resuscitation (EAR) 33, 47

fin swimming 4, 38, **38**, 47
finning 5, 7, 8, **9**
fins 7, **7**, **8**, 16, **16**, 19
fish 40, 41
floats 31, **31**, 35

goggles 7, 47

hyperventilation 14, 15, **15**, 47
hypothermia 12, 47

instruction 9, 42, 43, 46

knives 30, **30**

lens **6**, 7, 47
life jackets 22, **22**, 32, 44, 47
light 11
Lycra 20, 47

marine life 4, 5, 40, 41
mask clearing 24, **24**
mask fitting **16**, 17, 19
masks 4, 6, **6**, 8, 11, 17
monofilament line 30, 47
mushroom valve 18, 47

neoprene 7, 12, 21, 47
nitrogen 14, 47

octopush 4, 38, 47
oxygen 14, 15, 47

photography 5, 39
plankton 40, 41, 47
polymer 7, 47
pressure 10, 11, **11**, 26

reels 31, **31**

refraction 11, **11**, 47
rescue 32, 42
residual volume 15, **15**, 47
rolls 25, **25**
rotating bezel 31, 47

safety 5, 7, 14, 27, 34, 35, 43
self-help 32, **32**
shore cover 29, 33, 35
signals 28, **28**, 29, **29**, 35
sinuses 13, 47
snorkel clearing 19, **19**
snorkeling activities 38, 39
snorkels 4, 6, **6**, 18, **18**, 19
sound 11
"squid" 38, 47
subaqua diving 42
surface dives 4, 8, 26, **26**
surfacing 27, **27**

temperate waters 12, 21, 37, 47
tempered/toughened glass 7, 47
tidal streams 36, 47
tidal volume 15, **15**, 47
towing 33, **33**
training 5, 8, 33, 43, 46
tropical waters 20, 27, 36, 37, 40

useful tips 16

vacations 37
vision 11, **11**
vital capacity 15, **15**, 47
volume 11, **11**

watches 31
water 10
weather 36
weight belts 21, 23, **23**, **37**, 47
wetsuits 21, 32, 47

48